WITHDRAWN
FROM THE
PRATT INSTITUTE LIBRARY

D1127404

BY THE SAME AUTHOR

For Adults
Memory in a House

For Children
The Children of Green Knowe
The Chimneys of Green Knowe
The River at Green Knowe
A Stranger at Green Knowe
An Enemy at Green Knowe
The Sea Egg
Nothing Said

The Guardians of the House
(A MARGARET K. MC ELDERRY BOOK)

THE FOSSIL SNAKE

The
Fossil Snake

L. M. BOSTON

Illustrated by
Peter Boston

A MARGARET K. MCELDERRY BOOK

Atheneum 1976 *New York*

AC M

Library of Congress Cataloging in Publication Data
Boston, Lucy Maria, 1892-
The fossil snake.
"A Margaret K. McElderry book."
SUMMARY: *Rob puts the rare fossil of a coiled snake
he has discovered under the warm radiator in his
room. A wonderful thing happens.*
[1. Fantasy] I. Boston, Peter. II. Title.
PZ7.B6497Fo [Fic] 75-26997
ISBN 0-689-50037-8

Copyright © 1975 by L. M. Boston
Illustrations copyright © by Peter Boston
All rights reserved
Manufactured in the United States of America by
H. Wolff, New York
First American Edition.

For Charles
on his ninth birthday

———————

6/1/77

THE FOSSIL SNAKE

one

The truck stood in the yard loaded with stone that was to be used for building a wall. The young driver let down the flap and then winched up the body of the truck carelessly high, so that the stone shot down with a noise like a falling cliff.

"Idiot," said Rob's father. "You'll have smashed half of it."

"So what! Stone's stone."

"And rubble's rubble, but I ordered large pieces. Small bits are no good."

While his father was telling the driver just what he thought of him, Rob was clambering round the edge of the heap.

"Here's a splendid big piece broken in two."

"Careless idiot!" said his father as the truck was driven off.

"And look, Daddy, what's on the inside!"

Where the rock had split, on one surface was a raised shape like a coiled-up snake, on the other a hollow mould that had fitted over it.

"What can it be?"

"It's a fossil snake. Millions of years ago it was frozen in an ice age, buried in an avalanche perhaps, and then hundreds of thousands of years later there was a hot age with earthquakes and volcanoes of boiling rock, and the lava covered the frozen snake and turned into stone and afterwards there was another ice age and the rocks were cracked up and moved down by glaciers, and ultimately came to rest where they were quarried. And there it stayed till today when the stone was smashed. It's a wonderful specimen. Look, you can even see the patterns of the scales on its body."

Rob ran loving fingers round the diminishing coils.

"Can I keep it?"

"Yes, why not? You found it. Though I suppose we ought to give it to the Museum."

"No, no! You won't really?—Please let me have it. It's my special want."

"Yes, I said you could have it. We'll give the negative to the Museum."

All afternoon Rob helped his father to load stones onto a trolley and wheel them to the site of the wall. After tea they drove round to the Museum, taking both fossil stones to show the Director. The larger, heavier piece held the hollow shape, the actual fossil lay on a thin slab. Rob could easily carry it in his satchel.

At the office just inside the Museum door there was a tousled-looking young man with back street manners.

"Good afternoon," said Rob's father. "Where is my old friend Mr Porter? I hope he is not ill. Are you standing in for him?"

"He's retired. It's me now. What d'you want?"

"We would like to speak to the Director, please."

"He's busy. You'll have to wait."

"Will you tell him please that we are here? We'll wait in the fossil room. Come on, Rob. Let's go and see what fossils they have already. I'll be surprised if there is anything as good as ours. You could leave your satchel here in the office. It's heavy."

Rob gave one look at the young Curator and decided he'd sooner carry it.

They went into the gallery where the fossils were on show, case after case with minute pieces of black stone displayed behind glass. The young man having telephoned through to the Director followed them in, sticking close to them and listening to everything they said as if they might be thieves. Rob was hopping about in excitement.

"They haven't got anything nearly as good as ours."

His father pointed to a flat slab of stone covering most of a wall.

"What about that?" he said. In the middle of it, made while the rock was still hot and soft, was an immense print of a kind of hand, fantastic and horrible. The label underneath read,

Footprint of Megatherium

"Help!" said Rob. "What's that?"

"It's a giant beast. I don't know what it was, but it bounded across hot rock."

"It may be bigger than ours," said Rob, "but it's not as good. It's not a fossil at all."

At this point the Director came into the gallery to look for them. He knew Rob's father well.

"Yes, it's sad that we have lost old Porter. This is his nephew, Stephen, who we hope will learn to take his place. Actually, this is his first day, so he hasn't acquired the Institutional mannerisms yet." (A funny way, thought Rob's father, to say he is a lout.) "He's got a thing about fossils; that's really what got him the place. I hope he'll learn to appreciate the rest in time. It takes time."

"We have brought a fossil to show you, and another, not quite so good I'm afraid, to offer you. We left that one in the car because it's very heavy.

I mean, the stone is, that the fossil is in. We have the other here."

This was Rob's moment. He brought out his fossil snake and showed it to the Director. The young Curator's eyes showed white all round the iris like a madman's, and his enthusiasm overrode his manners so that he nosed in and jogged the Director's elbow.

"Careful, Stephen! You nearly made me drop it. My word! It is a beauty. We had better go into my study. Rob and I will go ahead, and perhaps you and Stephen will go and fetch the larger piece."

In the study the Director hummed and got out large catalogues of other museums one after another, flipping over pages, saying after each one,

"No; no; no. Ah! No."

When the other two returned carrying the stone with the hollow shape, he greeted them with the information, "There was one found in a quarry near Mousehole in 1884—let me see, where is it now?"

"Minneapolis Museum," prompted Stephen.

"Thank you, Stephen—I told you it was his subject—well now, Stephen, what do you think of these?"

Stephen swallowed hard. "Fine," he said.

The Director was extremely happy to accept the hollow stone. He asked what quarry it came from, what firm had supplied it, and what did they intend to do with the rest of the load. Then very gently but with overwhelming earnestness he suggested that the Museum ought to have both.

"You perhaps don't realise how rare these fossils are. Particularly the one your son has. Do you think it wise to entrust it to him? Boys are so careless."

Stephen put out his hand to it but Rob snatched it up off the table and hugged it to him, looking anxiously at his father.

"You gave it me," he said.

His father hesitated while Rob held his breath.

"I couldn't be so mean as to take it back when I've given it him."

"Perhaps the young gentleman will be so generous as to give it us himself?" said the Director, smiling persuasively.

Rob looked imploringly at his father.

"It's my greatest treasure," he said.

"I should think it is," said the Director. "It is worth a great deal of money, and has even more scientific value."

Stephen turned to Rob.

"Look here," he said, "suppose I gave you ten

13

pounds for it. Would that make a difference?"

The Director frowned and tapped on his desk.

"No, no, Stephen. I won't have that sort of dealing in this Museum. You know it could be worth much more."

"Yes, I do. But it ought to be in safe keeping." Stephen turned to Rob again.

"Where will you keep it, chum?" The impertinence of "chum" annoyed Rob.

"I'll take good care of it," was all he said, as he put it back in his satchel.

two

Rob was proud and overjoyed to have something so precious. Every time he looked at it or touched it, he was astonished at its mystery and perfection and at its unimaginable age. A thing like that must have magic. Things which came alive in the beginning of the world must have had enough energy bottled up in them to make everything else happen that developed from them afterwards.

He took the fossil upstairs to his bedroom. He wanted it to be a secret, and nobody else to see or touch it when he wasn't there, so he pushed it underneath the radiator. If it was a real snake it would like that, he thought. When they escaped from zoos they were always found in airing cupboards or among the hot pipes.

"There," he said, stroking it. "Have a nice warm up."

Then he thought he would go and look for more fossils. Who knows, he might find a fish, or a fern, or even the skeleton of a pterodactyl. But he found nothing else.

He had done a heavy day's work, so that after supper he shivered with tiredness.

"You'd better go to bed," said his mother. "It's coldish this evening. I'll turn the central heating up a little and you can be snug."

Before getting into bed, he pulled out the stone for a last look. It was warm on top, but underneath it was still cold. It must get warm right through before anything would happen, he found himself thinking.

The next day was like any other, but Rob was haunted by an undercurrent of excitement. At night he looked at his stone. It was warm all through. He put it carefully back.

"Hatch out, my lovely," he said, not knowing if he was pretending or believing. He hovered round it for a while, his heart beating. At last he got into bed.

He was just getting warm in bed and dropping off to sleep when he was startled by a slithering noise. It was not that it was loud, but it was not a sound he recognised. Could it have been his dressing gown slipping off the bed? No one would wake up for that. He switched on the light. The dressing gown was on the floor, so perhaps that was all. He went to sleep again, and not surprisingly dreamed of snakes.

17

It was a disturbed night. Never before had the mice made such a noise, scurrying and squeaking, and after their scutter above the ceiling just over his bed, there followed a very queer sound like someone softly stroking the joists with sandpaper. Rob lay wondering. The house felt different, as if something beside themselves had come to live in it. In the end he slept late and only woke when he was called to breakfast. His first act when he got out of bed was to look at his fossil. He pulled the stone out from under the radiator and was at first astonished and then enraged to see that there was no fossil snake, but only a shallow groove where it had been coiled. His father must have changed his mind and taken the fossil for the Museum and brought back the hollow mould to put in its place while he was asleep. How dared he? Rob was choking with anger, meaning to let fly at his father, but then he remembered that the Museum's piece was very much larger, that his father did not know where he had hidden the fossil and anyway he couldn't believe he would do a thing like that. He remembered the sounds in the night and slipped quietly back into his bedroom to think about it. While he was dressing, he decided it would be better not to say anything. It is always better to

have secret ideas. You never know what grown-ups will forbid.

At breakfast his mother said, "I must buy some mouse traps. I never heard such a chattering and squealing as they made last night. They sounded as if they'd all gone mad. Could there be a weasel in the house?"

"I never heard of weasels in houses but this one is so old perhaps they'd hardly recognise it as a house and mistake it for a quarry or part of the landscape. Lots of nice cracks everywhere."

"If it was a weasel, how would you catch it?"

"Why should you want to? It's catching mice for us. When it has eaten them all it will go hunting somewhere else."

Rob listened to this conversation between his parents with relief. He was glad that traps or poison would not be ordered, because he had his own notion of what was going on.

Just to make sure he asked carelessly, "What else eats mice beside weasels?"

"Owls and cats, but they'd hardly be under the floor boards." His father was eating, and answered between mouthfuls. "That goes for herons too. Hedgehogs would if they found a nestful of babies; dogs if they were starving; grass snakes, though I think they prefer frogs. Any kind of snake I daresay. Is there any more coffee, dear? Then I must get on with the wall. Rob, will you come and help?"

Rob nodded. "In a minute I will," and he went upstairs. Snakes he thought, like anything else, probably have favourite lairs. Where more likely than a warm dark place near the stone that had held it? He took his flashlight and lay down on the floor to look under the radiator. Curled up at the back against the wall was a bronze coloured snake, rather fatter than it had been as a fossil. Near it, where the pipe went down through the floor, was a hole that it could have squeezed though. It blinked sleepily at Rob and it did not occur to him to be afraid of it. It was his snake, and he had warmed it back to life. He was the companion of its lair. He hoped it would stay where it was and sleep off its first hunt after a million years. He wished he could freeze it up again when necessary, because it would never do for anyone else to see it.

"Hurry up Rob, I'm waiting," called his father.

Rob hung a wet towel over the radiator to make it more private, also steamy like the tropics, and hoped that would be what the snake would like. Then he had to go out. He worked all morning, very absent-mindedly, because of course he was

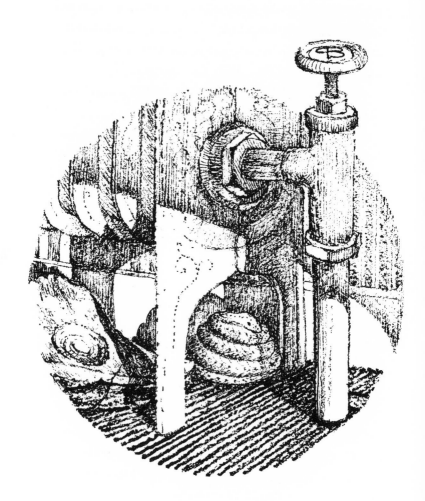

wondering a great many things. For instance, whether you could teach snakes anything, such as "Lie down and keep still", or if they were wilful and foolhardy. They were supposed to be very wily. It says in the Bible, "Wily as a Serpent."

"Hey Rob! Look alive, what are you thinking of?"

Rob was wondering what he should do if his father brought a friend to see his fossil. Had he better drop the stone in the river by-mistake-on-purpose?

He was free in the afternoon because his father had to go off in the car on business and his mother went too.

"Don't get into mischief," she said. "You'd better practise your recorder. We'll be back before dark."

Rob went up to look under the damp towel. The snake was safely there, its eyes glittering in the dark. It was coiled beside the stone as if to show that it claimed it as its personal property. Rob laughed to think what exciting company he had and nobody knew.

He sat on his bed and took his recorder. He belonged to a recorder club and was supposed to practise every day. Contentedly he began to play. After a skirmish up and down the scale to get going, he settled to practise his piece. He had not been playing very long when out of the corner of his eye he saw the towel over the radiator move slightly and a bronze head poked out.

"Oh, you like music, do you?" said Rob and played on. The head swayed from side to side in time to the tune, and gradually the whole length of snake glided out, and reared up in front of Rob, balancing itself on a couple of coils. Its head was level with his, its eyes level with his eyes. As the music went up and down so it swayed and danced, very controlled and mysterious, and Rob did not know if he was charming it or it was hypnotising him. He played on, because with the snake's eyes fixing him at close quarters like that, he was afraid to stop. At last he had to rest his lungs, and perhaps the snake had had enough of dancing for it subsided into coils, not with a visible winding movement as one would lay a rope, but in one flowing adjustment of its whole body. Being down, it laid its head for a moment on Rob's foot, then uncoiling with the same invisible motion—it just seemed to happen—it slid back into its lair.

Rob breathed again. One thing at least he knew now. It would come when he piped. He had better always have his recorder with him.

24

That night there were fewer squeals from the mice, and eventually silence in all the house, but in the early morning from the ivy outside Rob's window a terror broke out among roosting sparrows. Rob listened with some horror himself. It's *out*, he thought. What am I going to do with it? I'd better feed it with something to keep it quiet.

Next morning the snake was back beside its stone. It was growing hourly and could no longer fit into the grooves it once had made. Its colour was brightening from bronze to gold, and a faint pattern of green and rose was beginning to show all along its back. Rob decided to call it Ra.

Rob asked his mother if he could have an egg for breakfast. She said, "Yes, get one out of the egg basket." So Rob slipped it in his pocket, and she was so busy reading her letters she never noticed that he neither cooked nor ate it. It was taken up later to the snake, and gratefully received. Then Rob went down to help with building the wall.

"You're getting quite handy at this," said his father after a while.

"Do you think I'm worth twopence an hour?"

Rob was calculating that he would need extra pocket money for eggs and things.

"Yes I do. A very modest request."

three

Every afternoon when Rob was supposed to be practising his recorder he and the snake performed together, and as Rob played more easily, and with abandon, so his partner danced more snakily and with more authority, and always their eyes were level and fixed on each other. The coloured pattern of Ra's scales grew daily brighter. He was a very beautiful creature.

In the mornings the snake slept after his dawn hunting, and Rob helped his father with the wall. They were building it with earth instead of mortar, like a Cornish wall, planting roots between the stones as they went on, and taking great pleasure in it. It was going up fairly quickly, already three feet high.

One afternoon his parents both went off again. Their departing car was watched by a gang of rough youths who were idling on the river path beyond the wall. Among them was the young driver of the truck that had brought the stones. Rob was thinking that if the driver had not carelessly broken the piece of rock, he and his father would have built it into the wall with the fossil inside it, and Ra would never have been released. The driver seemed to be the leader of this gang. When the car was out of sight he said, in the half-shout which was the only way they talked, "Look at their snobby fancy wall. They must have something nobody else has got. We don't want a wall like that. We don't want a wall at all. There's never been one here. Let's knock it down. Throw their fancy wall in the river." At once with shouts of rude enjoyment they began to pull stones off the top and hurl them into the water.

"Hey!" said Rob who had been lying in the grass under a tree. "That's my Dad's wall. Leave it alone. He won't half be angry."

"He's not here," they answered, "and when he is here, we shan't be, so he can be as angry as he likes. We shan't half laugh." The wall was quickly being torn down by all of them working as if it was an important job.

"Stop," shouted Rob. "You can't do that. We built it ourselves."

"And we're unbuilding it, see?"

"I'll ring up the Police."

"Oh, you will, will you, you little scab! We'll

soon knock your teeth in so you can't talk."

They began to climb over, not very fast, because they stumbled and tripped on the heaps of stone lying ready for use on the garden side of the wall. Rob, desperately hoping, had just time to take up his recorder and begin to play. Before the first two, checked for a moment by his unexpected coolness, had reached him, out of the tree above him a golden, emerald and rose body was lowering itself and hung swaying with easy muscular strength, its head raised and steady.

"Flaming hell, look at that! Scram chaps, scram, clear out quick. I'm not waiting for any of that."

They all hurtled off, too frightened even to look round. The sound of their running boots was heard diminishing in the distance, and only when the motor bikes started up did the boasting and jeering begin again.

Ra meanwhile, descending from the tree, looped himself across Rob's shoulders and slid to the ground, ready for a dance. Fortunately, there was no one else about, so that Rob could let off his feelings in a swaying triumphant partnership. He played standing up, and Ra was now so long they were still face to face, so it went with a great swing. Afterwards he was able to pipe the snake into the

house and up to his bedroom, where he closed the window and the door. It had been a glorious rescue, but he was very worried. He did not think the boys would report to the Police that there was a snake abroad, because of what they themselves had done, but he feared they might be overheard talking, especially as their voices were so wild and loud. Perhaps he ought to tell his father, but you never knew with grown-ups. Even if his father let him keep Ra he was sure his mother wouldn't. He could not bear the idea of being parted from him.

When his father came back and saw the damaged wall, he was very angry. Rob told him all about it up to the point where he had said he would ring up the Police.

"And then they all went away."

"Well done, son. Did you recognise any of them?"

"Yes, the boy who brought the stones. But they weren't from here. They came on motor bikes."

"Confound the lot of them," said his father.

Nothing more was heard of them, and no rumours seemed to have got about. Ra, steadily growing, had an egg every morning to top off his hunting, and at the end of the week Rob had enough pocket money left to buy a very small rabbit from a farm boy who had been out shooting. He promised to let Rob have all the young ones that were no good for market.

"I suppose you want the skins," he said.

"Yes," Rob answered, lying manfully, "I'm making a model donkey for the crêche at Christmas."

He thought if Ra was well fed, he would lie quietly digesting, and be less likely to be seen. It was fascinating to watch the rabbit working down his long throat, and the more he fed Ra the closer their friendship would be. In fact Ra was finding his hiding place under the radiator too cramped. He took to sharing Rob's eiderdown with him in bed, until the dawn when he went hunting. Rob felt highly honoured.

four

His parents could not fail to notice that Rob's habits had altered. He was moody, secretive, always off by himself on some errand of his own. They asked him why he didn't have his friends in, and suggested picnics or ping-pong parties.

"No," he said. He was all right. He didn't want anybody.

"Why not? Isn't it more fun to have someone to do things with?"

"No, it isn't. They always interfere."

"That sounds rather selfish, dear."

"It isn't," said Rob, very hurt. "Some things are important." He made his escape and ran upstairs.

"What can he be up to?" said his mother.

"I've no idea. Perhaps a secret birthday present for you—or me. He seems to be saving up. He works like a beaver at the wall."

Rob began to hope his secret *could* be kept, though he did not know how far Ra's hunting excursions went. Ra always came back before anyone was stirring. He came in at the window, often wet, so Rob had to wash the wide dirty trail across his sill, and the bed-clothes were often inexplicably muddied. Rob always made his own bed—for a penny a day exacted from his mother—and covered the snake with the eiderdown before he left. It was a lazy creature and if well fed could be trusted to sleep for hours. The weather was bad, so there was less danger of its going out to sun itself in the garden. The Easter holidays were almost over. School was going to bring more problems for Rob.

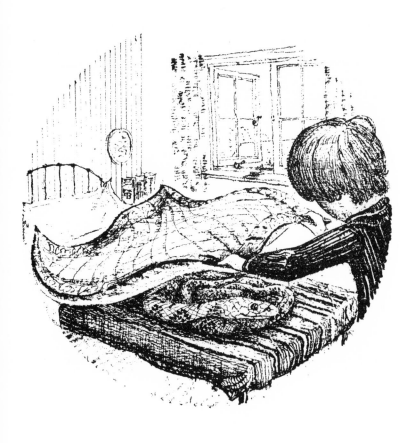

five

One night as Rob and Ra lay together in bed, two things happened at the same moment to disturb him. A slight shift in the coils beside him suggested that Ra was going hunting, while a rustling and cracking in the ivy under the window suggested that something was climbing in. Unmistakably human grunts and panting made this clearer. Rob's bed was right under the window. He lay rigid, putting his arm around Ra for reassurance. It was very dark, nothing could be seen in the black square of night, but something could be heard to heave up and rest on the sill. After a moment the bright beam of a flashlight shone into the room. It wavered a little, high on the wall opposite, and then was purposefully lowered to sweep round. The first thing it lit up was Ra weaving about making a terrible shadow behind him, that filled the wall and half the ceiling; but when the light actually focused on him, he was close to the intruder and drawn up to strike, the beam of the flashlight glancing back off his bright metallic head. There was a gasp of fear, the flashlight fell into the room and there was a sound of torn ivy followed by a dull thud, then silence. Rob leapt out of bed, picked up the flashlight and shone it down out of the window. He saw a figure slumped on the ground, which tried to escape from the light by crawling away on hands and knees, with groans and stifled squeaks of pain. From above it was not easy to recognise someone in that position, but it looked like the young man from the Museum. He wanted to steal my fossil, thought Rob, but he found what he didn't expect! As this was a dangerous subject that might lead to questions, it would be wiser to say nothing about the attempted theft. Rob's room was at the back of the house and his parents' at the front. Luckily nobody else seemed to have heard anything.

Next morning the postman reported that the young man at the Museum had broken his ankle—"Skidded on his motor bike or something—must have been drunk, for he can't give a clear account of anything." Rob was the only person not surprised, but he was very pleased. He sent Stephen in hospital a postcard on which he drew a fossil, writing "I know you like snakes."

His mother said, "That's kind of you dear, I expect he'll be pleased."

six

In the end someone must have talked, because the village suddenly was full of rumours of snakes. Farmers lost their chickens. Dogs howled at night, cattle stampeded. And then the dreaded day came when police arrived at the house to see Rob's father.

"I wonder if you can help us, sir. There's a lot of panic in the village about a snake said to be seen in your garden. Have you by any chance got such a creature, that might escape from wherever you keep it? Generally when there's a panic there's a reason of some sort for it, though mostly exaggerated."

"Yes, we have a snake," his father answered, much amused. "But it's a fossil! I expect someone perhaps at the Museum said we had a fossil snake, and the next person said a snake, leaving out the fossil—and there you are. After that everything that happens is due to the snake."

"I daresay you're right, sir. People are so silly. From what they say it would be a monstrous big one, and that's hardly likely."

However, a few days later on a Saturday, the policeman came back again bringing a little wizened man whom he introduced as Professor Scales who was staying at the Pie and Eel. The professor apologised for intruding, but snakes were his subject. The reports he had heard in the bar of the pub about this real or imaginary snake were so extraordinary, so unlike any known snakes and so suggestive of a variety considered as extinct as the mammoth, that he was intensely interested, the more so as in the early morning when the dew was on the grass, he had distinctly seen the mark left by the passage of a large reptile. In the interests of Science he wondered if he might be allowed to put a baited trap somewhere in the garden.

"What's a snake trap like?" asked Rob. He controlled his horror as well as he could, but his voice trembled. However, this was a subject that might be expected to excite any boy.

"It's a close-knit wire cage with an opening the snake could just get through," said the Professor, his hands lovingly showing the size and shape as he talked. "Inside you put a young pig. As you know perhaps, a snake's jaws are not fixed like ours but can come apart and stretch to any size. The snake swallows the pig whole, and then of course, it can't get out of the small opening where it came in, and we can either kill it, or give it to the Zoo. If this one is what I am daring to hope—I have seen the fossil you gave to the Museum, and from the pattern of the scales I think this might be the same species, and if so of immense, *of immense* interest—if so, I say it would probably be best to kill it for dissection, and have the skin stuffed for the Natural History Museum."

He evidently had a great deal to say, but Rob had heard enough. He backed out and ran.

"I expect he's gone to fetch his fossil for you," said his father. "He's madly jealous of it. You are really being honoured." He showed the talkative old gentleman into the sitting room.

Rob didn't waste a minute. Ra had only just been fed with a rabbit, so was sluggish and contented. Rob wound him round and round his body and looped the head over his shoulder; then he put on his jacket with the string well tightened round his body, to prevent Ra slipping down, the front zipped up. He took the fossil stone in a basket and slipped out of the back door while the Professor was still holding forth very learnedly about snakes he had known.

Rob's first idea was the church. It was Saturday

and most people would be away on their weekend sport or pleasures, or on the river. He might get to the church without being noticed and no one would look for him there. He could sit inside safely and think out what to do next. The way was rather steeply uphill, but he got there without meeting anybody and gladly sat down in a pew near the door, for Ra was heavy and now and again tightened a coil round his ribs so that it was hard to breathe. Once he had settled down, the coils loosened and shifted and he could feel Ra's head nuzzling in the hair at the back of his neck.

At first it seemed absolutely quiet in the church, but presently Rob, and doubtless Ra too, began to hear little noises, clicks, clinks, soft taps, bumps and movings, all seeming vague and unconnected. There was a crash of something knocked over. The vestry door was opened and the parson appeared, propping himself against the door post. He was a little untidy man with a face like a strawberry. He was very tender-hearted and nobody could dislike him, but it was a village joke that he drank too much. Not of course in the pub, but in his lonely vicarage. He shuffled unsteadily in, muttering to himself. He tripped on the coconut matting, steadied himself on the front pew, swerved uncertainly

towards the chancel steps and corrected himself to bear right. He had a glass in one hand and some papers in the other, and appeared to be trying to get himself to the lectern. There the papers slipped off the book to the floor. He wanted to pick them up, but found nowhere to put his glass down and stood waving it vaguely about and muttering. Finally, he put it on the chancel steps and unsteadily retrieved his papers. Rob supposed he was trying to mark in the big Bible the lesson for Sunday morning, but it was beyond him. He pushed the pages backwards and forwards and said, "Eshjekiel's not in thish. Ish been lef' out." He shut the Bible impatiently and turned to an imagined congregation.

"Can't read the leshon. Eshjekiel's been lef' out."

At this point he saw that there was a congregation of one, and his mouth fell open. Rob had felt a movement between his neck and his collar, and realised that Ra was rising up. The parson fell on his knees and began to pray desperately for forgiveness and mercy, no less earnestly because his speech was blurred and his tongue would not obey him.

"Acknowlish my shinge and the weaknesh of my flesh but let not the devil si' in the congregation before me. Let not the devil ge' get me." He fell forward hiding his eyes and wept loudly.

45

Rob took his chance and slipped out of the door, pulling the hood of his jacket over his own head and Ra's.

"You inquisitive old thing! What possessed you to stick your head out just then?"

He had to laugh—but where now?

He had a secret place of his own further up the hill where nobody went, or at least he had never met anyone there, and had never shown it to any of his friends. It was a hard scramble up to it through a scruffy little wood rooted in broken stone and tangled with bramble, no place to tempt people for walks or picnics, but at the top there was a flat rock in full sun, and under the rock a deep crack that seemed the mouth of a small cave. The opening was too small for a boy to squeeze in, but there was no knowing how far it went into the earth. He had often lain with his ear to the crack believing he could hear echoes of running water far away. An underground stream must come out somewhere. Perhaps it was the one that ran through his own distant garden into the river.

By this secret place, Rob, with great relief, took off his jacket and released Ra. He placed the stone that he had carried all this time in the cave as far as he could reach, to mark that this was Ra's lair.

Then he lay flat on the rock in the sun to rest while Ra coiled beside him, keeping his head raised as if on sentry duty, with the tops of trees below him all round.

As the sun began to go down, and all the world went rosy red, the painful time came when Rob must separate himself from Ra. He talked to him and fondled him, for his own pleasure, more than for the pleasure of this kingly creature, who was independent and had his own ways. He explained to him that this was where he was now to live, marked by his own stone, and that Rob would visit him often.

They did a melancholy goodbye dance together. Then as Rob put his recorder under his pullover, Ra subsided with that wonderful liquid smoothness that was all muscle, and slid away into his cave. When the last zigzag of the tail withdrew out of sight, Rob turned with tears and began to stumble down through the wood and so homeward, where no gorgeous secret would ever again be waiting in his room.

seven

It isn't always easy to break away from the plans of one's family, even at weekends, but as the days grew longer, Rob found time for the long climb to his secret place. He tried to go a slightly different way each time, so as never to make an obvious track that might tempt other boys to explore. He always took an offering with him, and his heart never failed to leap with joy when in answer to his piping, that sovereign head appeared out of the crack in the rock.

In one of those unexpected cold nights in May, he even woke up to find Ra with him under the eiderdown. So he knew his way down! Would it be along the ledges where the little stream led from the cave to the garden? Perhaps he went far afield. After that, Rob, when out alone, would often get out his recorder, just in case, and sometimes a ripple would run through a field of hay and Ra would appear, or out of the middle of a haystack against which Rob was leaning in the sun, or at twilight, under the evening star, from the reeds round the mill pond.

Once at midsummer Rob woke up with the white light of the full moon lying across his face and his pillow. His room looked magical and he longed for Ra. He got out of bed and leant out of the window. The garden was full of a strange milky light. It looked much bigger than in daylight. He could say —*that* is the path, the wall, the gate, the yew tree— but it was hard to believe. It looked like something he was dreaming. Where the house or a tree threw a shadow, it did not look like the flow of light merely interrupted by some known thing, it looked like black night showing through the thin crust of a dream. This surely was fairy land.

Rob dressed and climbed out of his window down the thick ivy where Ra had come and gone— and Stephen too—and began to walk along the lane to the church. Everywhere was so quiet and empty there might be no other human beings alive. The big trees along the hedge cast shadows so total that Rob was unsure whether he would bump into them or step suddenly into nothingness. The silence seemed to sing, and his steps rang over the country-side. It was reassuring, when he ventured to walk into one of the most secretive shadows, to hear his footfall make so hard a thud on the solid earth.

He passed the church which huddled in the

shadows of its buttresses as if trying to shut out so pagan a light. Its roof and tower were bathed in silver, but behind every tombstone was a black hole into the underworld. It was all as eerie as it was beautiful.

It was when Rob reached the wooded hill that his real difficulties began. The moonlight was bright over all the upper surface of the trees, but underneath it only penetrated in streaks and little circles of light that made recognition of what was there far more difficult. Rob had brought a flashlight but when he shone it before him it picked out great arching barriers of brambles set with steely thorns, but could not show how dense they were. The only way was to keep on going uphill wherever he could find space to pass, but sometimes he would feel as if he was wrapped around and trapped altogether and would never tear himself free. At last he broke out into a bare scaley patch that he knew, and after that he had but to clamber from one bent hawthorn to the next, jerking his clothes free from thorns and burrs, till at last, torn and scratched and panting, he was at the top.

By now the moon was high overhead, bright as could be in the silky blue sky, dazzling on the flat stone that reflected it.

Ra was at home. He rose up as Rob stepped onto the stone. The movements of his arrogant-eyed wedge-shaped head seemed to claim that all this glory was his own, and indeed Rob gasped as he looked round at the wide familiar view so transformed.

The two of them had a ritual to perform, and this was surely the place and the time for it. The notes of the recorder sounded like the horns of Elfland as they travelled out across the flood of unearthly light in which Ra's burnished scales as he moved backwards and forwards glittered like phosphorescence on the crest of a smooth swell. Rob, ecstatically swaying too, as he piped, realised in his heart with more pride than regret that this would be their last dance. Ra had become too big for him, too awe-inspiring, too much akin to this overwhelming moonlight. It was as if he had gone back to his own time, when the moon was so much bigger and brighter than it is now.

MRS. BOSTON *lives in a house near Cambridge, England that was built in the twelfth century, a house that is known to readers all over the world as Green Knowe, the setting of nearly all her books. She writes only in the winter, for during the summer she spends all her working time in her garden where she grows many kinds of old roses as well as other sweet-smelling flowers.*

Mrs. Boston has four grandchildren and one son, Peter, who has illustrated most of her books, including The Fossil Snake.

ACM   cop.1

Boston
    The fossil snake

PRATT INSTITUTE LIBRARY

This book due on the last date stamped below.
Fine of TEN CENTS per day thereafter.

DUE   DUE
_____

MAY 1 6 1978

SEP 1 2 1981 REC'D

MAR 3 1 1994

APR 4 REC'D